W9-AXT-703

WILEY & GRAMPA'S CREATURE FEATURES
MONSTER FISH FRENZY

WRITTEN AND ILLUSTRATED BY

KIRK SCROGGS

DEEP-FRIED TERROR AWAITS!

LITTLE, BROWN AND COMPANY

New York · Boston

This book is in memory of Sam Smith,
master boater and joke teller.

———————

Special thanks—

Suppasak Viboonlarp; Mark Mayes; Jackie Greed; Alejandra; Neil and
Debbie and Kai Gowensmith; Jim Jeong; the mezz crew woo woo!

Andrea, Sangeeta, Saho, Alison and the Little, Brown Crew—yippy!

Mike, Deborah and Dante Parker;
An extra-gassy special thanks to Dav Pilkey.

And an extra crusty thanks to Ashley & Carolyn Grayson and Dan Hooker
And Diane and Corey Scroggs

Copyright © 2006 by Kirk Scroggs

Little, Brown and Company

Hachette Book Group USA
1271 Avenue of the Americas, New York, NY 10020
Visit our Web site at www.lb-kids.com

First Edition: October 2006

Library of Congress Cataloging-in-Publication Data

Scroggs, Kirk.
   Monster fish frenzy/written and illustrated by Kirk Scroggs.—1st ed.
     p. cm.—(Wiley & Grampa's creature features; #3)
   Summary: While Grampa and Wiley try to capture the legendary Moby Fizz, the "biggest,
bloated, deformed bass" in Lake Putrid, they encounter many surprises.
   ISBN-13: 978-0-316-05944-2 (hc) / ISBN-10: 0-316-05944-7 (hc)
   ISBN-13: 978-0-316-05945-9 (pb) / ISBN-10: 0-316-05945-5 (pb)
   [1. Grandparents—Fiction. 2. Fishes—Fiction. 3. Humorous stories.] I. Title.

PZ7.S436726Mo 2006
[Fic]—dc22

2006040814

10 9 8 7 6 5 4 3 2 1

CW

Printed in the United States of America

Series design by Saho Fujii

The illustrations for this book were done in Staedtler ink on Canson Marker paper,
then digitized with Adobe Photoshop for color and shade.
The text was set in Humana Sans Light and the display type was handlettered.

CHAPTERS

1. Sounds Fishy to Me 1
2. Tentacle Lickin' Good 8
3. The Tail of Moby Fizz 17
4. A Vord of Varning! 25
5. Yo Ho Ho and a Bucket of Chum 28
6. Bubble Trouble 35
7. Piranha Point 36
8. Tail of Destruction 42
9. As the Worm Turns 45
10. An Imperfect Storm 50
11. Take It from a Big Mouth 52
12. Captain's Log 57
13. The Island of Lost Hippies 61
14. Extreme Boat Makeover 66
15. Big Mouth Strikes Again! 69
16. A Pleasant Development 76
17. Hanging Around Fish Organs 80
18. Sayonara Robo-carp! 89
19. Will the Real Moby Fizz Please Stand Up? 92
20. Reunited and It Feels So Slimy 97

CRACKPOT SNAPSHOT 102

CHAPTER 1

Sounds Fishy to Me

Ladies and Gentlemen, you are about to encounter a species of fish thought to be extinct for 65 million years—Big Bassosaurus Rex. It weighs approximately 6 tons. That's 2,650,003 fish sticks for all you less-educated people out there. If you meet up with this fish, do not make any sudden movements, and whatever you do, never call it cruel names like Blubber Butt or Big Lips Pooperstink! Proceed with extreme caution!

Don't get scared yet! That's not the bloated, bloodshot eye of a monster kid-eating fish!

That's just Paco, Grampa's prize pet goldfish. And that's me, Wiley, filming Grampa and Paco for *America's Most Talented Animals*.

"Please observe," I said quietly, "as Grampa feeds Paco his favorite cuisine, Pork Cracklins."

Paco's even crazier for Pork Cracklins than Grampa is. In fact, he can detect Cracklins from miles away and he'll do anything for those succulent pork bits.

He can leap through sizzling beer-battered onion rings.

He can play dead.

He even does a mean Elvis!

"I wish you two wouldn't go on about that fish!" complained Gramma. "You're gonna upset Merle! After all, he's a talented animal, too. Just look at him!"

"You're right, Granny," said Grampa. "But he's
no match for this fish. Paco's gonna make us so
rich we'll blow our noses on $100 bills! The
world will be our oyster!"

"Oyster!" I shouted, interrupting Grampa's loony rambling. "I almost forgot! It's All-You-Can-Eat Fried Oyster & Waffle Night at the Crustacean Plantation! We've only got two hours left!"

Tentacle Lickin' Good

Crustacean Plantation, Gingham County's swankiest seafood restaurant, was filled to the brim with satisfied diners.

We were met at the door by Captain Gerald, the one-handed owner of the restaurant.

"Ahoy there!" said Captain Gerald. "You fine folks sit right down and make yerselves at home while we stuff your bellies with the finest deep-fried marine critters this side of the Gulf of Mexico!"

The food was squidliscious! Gramma and I got started on the oysters and waffles while Grampa had an octopus salad with zesty ranch dressing.

"Hey, that reminds me," I said. "In school today, we learned that a sea cucumber is the only creature that can spit up its internal organs and then grow new ones."

"Wiley!" said Gramma, shocked and sickened. "Not while we're eating!"

"Yeah!" said Grampa, a ranch-drenched tentacle hanging out of his mouth. "What are you trying to do? Gross us out?"

"Can I get ye some more fried oysters and waffles?" asked Captain Gerald.

"Ye sure can," I said, "with extra syrup!"

"Shiver me timbers!" said Captain Gerald. "I haven't seen an appetite like yours since the fish that swallowed me hand!"

I was intrigued. "You mean..."

"Moby Fizz!" gasped everyone in the restaurant at the same time.

"Moby Fizz!" said Crusty O'Hoolihan, local fisherman. "That fish was burped up from the bowels of purgatory! Big as a double-wide trailer and twice as mean!"

"That cursed fish ate my pet poodle, Dinky!" said Marjorie Millner, local old person. "He went out for a dog paddle and I never saw him again!"

"Aaay!" continued Captain Gerald. "One minute I'm synchronized swimming with the boys, the next, I'm in the hospital with one hand missin'. There's only one man who's laid eyes on Moby Fizz and still has all of his limbs. In fact...

he's sitting right there!"

"What, what?" Grampa said, jolted out of his nap. "Is it time for dessert?"

"We wanna hear about Moby Fizz!" I said.

"Moby Fizz! Moby Fizz! Moby Fizz!" we all chanted, banging our maple-syrup dispensers on the table.

"All right! All right!" Grampa said. "The tale I'm about to tell you is so secret and personal that I've never told it to anyone other than all my friends and family at every social gathering for the last seventy-five years."

CHAPTER 3

The Tail of Moby Fizz

GRAMPA AGE 7

"It all started many, many years ago when I was a tiny ragamuffin, no taller than a bag of grain. Today, you know me as Grampa, but back then, people called me Ishmael."

"I thought they called you Little Stinker," said Gramma.

"Don't interrupt me, Granny," said Grampa. "Call me Ishmael."

"One day, I decided to prove my manhood and embark on a solo fishing voyage. Just me and the open water… and my favorite stuffed animal, Captain Froggy, of course. We set out on a little wooden dinghy into the heart of Lake Putrid. The swells were about 5 feet, the wind was at 10 knots, and my hair was looking particularly stylish.

"Everything was going wonderfully…

that is, until we were attacked by the biggest,
most bloated, most deformed bass the world has
ever known! In one gulp it swallowed us up—
boat, frog—the whole enchilada!

"So there we were, stuck inside of a monster fish with the million other things he had swallowed.

'Well, this is it, Captain Froggy,' I said. 'We're done for! Doomed to be digested in a fish's gut for all eternity! This is sure gonna look silly on our tombstones.'

"Lucky for us, Moby had swallowed a shipment of carbonated, fizzy water on its way to a circus-clown colony on the North Shore. I shook every one of those bottles of fizzy water until they exploded, filling the air in Moby's stomach with carbon dioxide gas. Pretty soon the fish started to bloat and rumble until...

Moby Fizz let out the biggest release of natural gas since The Great Texas Chili Cook-Off of 1907! The burp blew me clear out over Lake Putrid.

"But Captain Froggy didn't make it. He was caught on Moby's teeth like a piece of spinach. Those blubbery fish lips closed on Froggy and he slipped down beneath the waves never to be seen again.

"I floated for days until I was rescued by the Gingham County female waterskiing team, the Ladies of the Lake. A small, round girl about my age carried my withered, little body as we skied back to shore.

"And that," concluded Grampa, "was the first time I laid eyes on Gramma and we began our life together, which is another tale of terror entirely that we don't have time to get into right now."

The crowd was stunned by Grampa's story.

"Death to Moby Fizz!" screamed Crusty O'Hoolihan.

"Avenge my poodle!" demanded Marjorie Millner.

"Where are my waffles?!" shouted a disgruntled diner.

"Aaaay!" said Captain Gerald. "Let's have ourselves a little contest! I'll offer a king's bounty to whoever finds Moby Fizz! Dead or alive or deep-fried—let's go fishin'!"

CHAPTER 4

A Vord of Varning!

"Leave ze fish be," said a creepy voice. It was Dr. Hans Lotion and his grandson, Jurgen. "If you disturb zat fish, it vill bring grave misfortune on Gingham County. It vill eat your children as if zey vere tangy, chewy gummy bears!"

We all took Dr. Lotion's warning very seriously.

"Did I mention I'll throw in free all-you-can-eat fried oysters and waffles?" said Captain Gerald.

The next day, everyone in town showed up at Lake Putrid to hunt Moby Fizz. My best friend, Jubal, joined our team and Gramma packed us some of her world-famous pimento and cheese sandwiches.

"Pimento and cheese! Thanks, Granny," said Grampa. "We can use it to plug up any leaks should we start sinking!"

The contestants prepped their boats and checked their gear and fish weaponry.

Even Grampa's hounds, Esther and Chavez, got in on the action.

CHAPTER 5

Yo Ho Ho and a Bucket of Chum

Spirits were high as we set forth on our grand adventure! First, we did an equipment check.

Life jackets—
check!

Assorted hooks, tackle,
and slimy bait—check!

One vat of chum made
from fish guts, rotten
eggs, buttermilk, and
horseradish—check!

"Um!" said Grampa, smacking his lips. "This chum's not half bad! Kinda tastes like one of your Gramma's power smoothies!"

"I heard that!" yelled Gramma from the shore.

"Grampa," I said, pulling out a rather scary-looking map...

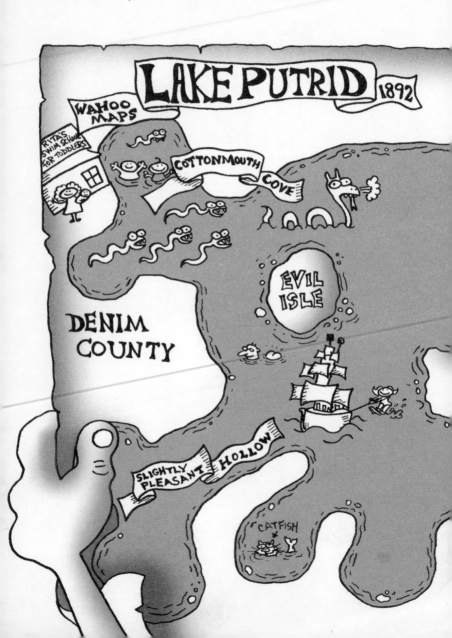

"before we get too far, there are some areas on this map of Lake Putrid that we should definitely avoid like…"

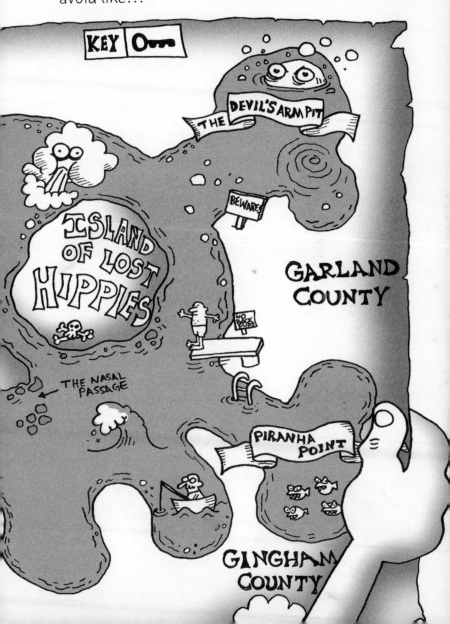

"Maps shmaps!" said Grampa. "I've been lost on this lake dozens of times for days on end and I never needed a map! Why, I can just sniff the wind and follow my nose and it will lead us straight to that stinky beast!"

So Grampa sniffed the wind and his nose led us straight to...

It was Vera, Gingham Elementary's world-renowned lunch lady and master food poisoner!

"What are you doing here?" I asked, horrified.

"Oh, hello, sweety!" Vera replied. "I'm just gathering algae and water bugs for Monday's lunch special. I call it Sweet and Sour Seafood Surprise."

"I gotta remember to pack my lunch," said Jubal.

Vera whipped out an electronic contraption. "I have to warn you boys. My Electromagnetic Radar Fish Detector thingy's picked up a large mass in these waters."

"Wow!" I said. "She's got an Electromagnetic Radar Fish Detector thingy!"

"You don't need a fancy gizmo to find Moby," said Grampa. "Ever since my little fizzy water incident, Moby's been gassier than an Exxon station. All you gotta do is watch for the bubbles. If you see bubbles, you got troubles!"

Putrid Pearl

Bubble Trouble

All of a sudden, the water churned with bubbles and Moby Fizz surfaced beneath Vera! Moby stared at us with an eye as big as a trampoline.

"We're gonna need a bigger boat," I said.

"And a lot of tartar sauce!" added Jubal.

Piranha Point

As quickly as he had appeared, Moby swam away. But Vera had been knocked overboard!

"Holy mackerel!" I shouted, pulling out my map. "If my calculations are correct, we're in Piranha Point! Legend has it that a disgruntled pet store employee released a piranha in this cove years ago and now the place is teeming with them! We've got to get her out of the water! A school of piranha can devour a water buffalo in sixty-five seconds!"

"Wow!" said Jubal. "It takes me at least ten minutes!"

"That piranha business is just an old wives' tale!" said Grampa. "Look, I'll put my hand in the water and nothing will happen!"

"Okay," said Grampa, "maybe swimming isn't such a good idea!"

Unfortunately, a school of piranha had already homed in on Vera's splashing and was heading her way!

"We've got to do something!" shouted Jubal.

He was right. I had to act fast.

So I pushed Jubal into the lake!

"Hey, piranha!" I shouted. "Come over here! Eat my friend instead! He's got a lot more meat on his bones and he's low in polysaturated fats!"

The school of piranha fell for it and changed course. Now they were heading directly toward Jubal!

At the last minute, just as the little beasties were about to sink their teeth into Jubal's soft hide, I tossed one of Gramma's pimento and cheese sandwiches into the lake.

The piranha went for the sandwich while Jubal and Vera climbed onboard. Everyone was safe and sound.

Except for the piranha. They didn't survive the pimento and cheese sandwich.

"I'll never underestimate the power of your Gramma's cooking again," said Grampa.

"I heard that!" yelled Gramma from the shore.

CHAPTER 8

Tail of Destruction

"Toodles!" said Vera as we departed. "Thanks for rescuing me! I'm gonna make you a special dish for lunch on Monday!"

"You shouldn't!" I yelled back. "Really, you shouldn't!"

As we headed deeper into Lake Putrid, we saw that Moby Fizz had left a trail of total devastation. The other contestants and their boats were in shambles!

We floated up to Nate Farkles, clinging to all that was left of his boat—his prize collection of ceramic penguins.

"I don't know what happened," said Nate. "All I did was throw a razor-sharp harpoon at Moby Fizz and he goes and destroys my boat!"

"Hang in there!" said Grampa. "Help is on the way! I wish we could help, but this boat's reached maximum weight capacity. Besides, I've got a monster fish to find and a stuffed frog to avenge!"

CHAPTER 9

As the Worm Turns

Moments later, we heard a sickening slurping noise.

"Stop the boat!" I said. "Shhhhhhh! Listen."

"It's Moby Fizz!" said Jubal. "He's found us!"

But the slurping seemed to be coming from the ice cooler, and it was getting louder and slurpier.

Grampa reached over slowly and pulled off the lid to find...

It was Merle, and he was slurping up earthworms like fettuccine Alfredo!

"A stowaway!" exclaimed Grampa. "In the pirate days, this sneaky varmint would've had to walk the plank for this!"

"I don't think Gramma would like that," I said.

As time went by, Grampa became more and more determined to find Moby Fizz. He just wasn't himself. He got all whiskery and disheveled and wasn't gonna stop until he found that fish.

It was hard on us kids, too. The labor was back-breaking, the sun beat down on us with no mercy, food was scarce, and scurvy was setting in!

"I can't believe we've only been out here for two hours," said Jubal.

And as if things couldn't get any worse, Blue Norther, channel 5's smarmy weatherman, appeared on Grampa's portable combo T.V./radio/toaster/espresso maker.

"Hi, folks! Our Whopper Doppler radar's picked up a northern front from Iceland and this swirlylooking cloud thing from Peru. If these two systems collide it'll probably be real bad. So stay inside and stay off Lake Putrid! In the next few minutes, that lake will become a churning, swirling death trap! Have a wonderful day!"

"Grampa," I pleaded, "you heard Blue Norther.
This dinky little boat can't withstand a thunder-
storm, let alone a swirly cloud thing from Peru!
Let's head back to shore!"

"Absolutely not!" said Grampa. "I'd brave a Gale
7 hurricane, a sea of burning oil, a swarm of
killer bees…why, I'd even trim my nose hairs
with a rusty Weedwacker before I'd give up
Moby Fizz!"

"Wow! That's dedication," said Jubal.

CHAPTER 10

An Imperfect Storm

Blue Norther was right. The two storms collided directly over us just as we were entering the most dangerous part of Lake Putrid—The Devil's Armpit!

"Maybe we should put on our life jackets," I suggested.

"Don't be silly," said Grampa. "I've nearly drowned in storms dozens of times and I never needed a life jacket!"

DANGER: SHARP ROCKS!

CHAPTER 11
Take It from a Big Mouth

Before we knew it, we were face-to-face with the mother of all monster fish, Moby Fizz!

"Wiley!" Grampa bellowed. "Hold her steady! Jubal, prepare the net!"

"I don't think he's gonna fit in this net!" said Jubal.

"He will when I get through with him!" said Grampa, raising his harpoon.

But before Grampa could throw the harpoon—
Whap! Moby used our little boat to practice his
power serve! We were plunged into the icy
depths of Lake Putrid.

Beneath the water I was tossed around by the current like a pair of dirty drawers in a giant washing machine.

I was about to black out when I noticed something strange and horrifying—I could see Moby
Fizz skimming the bottom of the lake and he
was sporting a big, grotesque appendage that
was sucking up fish by the hundreds. This thing
truly was a monster!

CHAPTER 12

Captain's Log

I gathered my strength and swam to the surface, where I found the others floating on a stray log.

"Nice of you to join us, Wiley," said Grampa. "We were just kickin' it. Tellin' a few knock knock jokes."

After a while, the storm clouds cleared and the waters were calm again.

That is, until suddenly, the water around us began to churn with bubbles!

"Oh no!" I yelled. "The bubbles! Moby's back for seconds!"

"Actually, that was me," said Grampa. "I never should have had that second can of chili for breakfast."

So, Jubal, Merle, and I got our own log.

Soon, night fell and we drifted off to sleep. My slumber was troubled by nightmares and visions.

In my dreams I saw
Grampa, transformed into
a grizzled old Captain
Ahab, obsessed with
avenging Captain Froggy.

I saw Gramma
desperately
searching for her
missing loved
ones.

And I saw myself, ruling over
a colony of tiny talking pickles
who worshiped me like a
Greek god. (This part
has nothing to do
with anything,
but I thought it
was pretty
cool anyway.)

CHAPTER 13

The Island of Lost Hippies

We awoke to find ourselves in grass skirts, surrounded by smiling hippies!

"Don't worry, kids," said the head hippie. "Your clothes are drying by the fire."

"If I'd known I was going to be wearing a grass skirt in public, I would have hit the gym first," Jubal said, embarrassed.

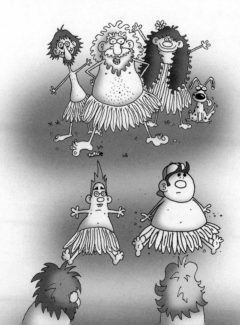

"These things are pretty comfy," said Grampa, "and they're great for hula dancing!"

"Ughhh!" I groaned. The sight of Grampa in a skirt was just too much for my young eyes!

"You're on the Island of Lost Hippies," said a girl hippie known as Earth Mother. "Tall, short, round, skinny—we all wear grass skirts. No one should be ashamed...

except for Artie, of course. I mean, that's just wrong."

So we gathered around the campfire in our skirts, and roasted marshmallows and drank root beer floats. Grampa entertained the hippies with the story of Moby Fizz.

Later that night I had a heart-to-heart with Earth Mother.

"Earth Mother," I said, "I'm worried about Grampa. He's not himself. He only thinks of catching Moby Fizz and nothing else."

"Your grampa is plagued by the past," she said. "Confront this mighty fish he must. Just look at him. He's been sitting on that cliff for hours, staring out at the open water, waiting for the moment he can take on the scaly beast and move on with his life."

Actually, Grampa was napping.

CHAPTER 14

Extreme Boat Makeover

In the morning, the hippies woke us with a surprise. They had found our boat and repaired it while we slept!

"First we sealed the leaks with tree sap and acorns," said the head hippie, "then we coated the entire boat with a protective layer of snail mucus."

"Then we added a 1,200 horsepower Liquijet 5000 jet-boat engine with a magnetron electronic ignition, outboard hydraulic tilt and trim, and a twist-grip throttle."

"Wow!" I said. "Where did you get that?"

"Oh, on the other side of the island," said Earth Mother. "There's a Manny's Boat World next to that veggie-burger joint."

After bidding a sad farewell to our new hippie friends, we took off once again in search of the elusive Moby Fizz.

"Look at those nutty hippies," said Grampa. "They're waving their hands, dancing around and screaming like crazy people. How cute."

CHAPTER 15

Big Mouth Strikes Again!

So we waved back and jetted off, straight into the open mouth of Moby Fizz!

At least, I thought it was Moby Fizz. The inside
of the fish was all shiny and there were lights
and signs and some soothing smooth jazz play-
ing over a loudspeaker.

"Wow!" exclaimed Grampa. "They've really done
a lot with this place! It used to be so...slimy."

"This isn't a real fish," I said. "It's some sort of—"

"Submersible android fish research vessel, to be exact!" said a familiar voice. It was Dr. Hans Lotion and his grandson, Jurgen. "I call it Robo-carp! You must forgive me for attacking you yesterday. Ze Robo-carp mistook you for an enemy threat."

"So what do you do on this tub of bolts, Doc?" asked Grampa.

"Come, I vill show you."

"Ze fish shape of zis vehicle allows us to con-
duct our studies vithout disturbing ze natural
habitat of Lake Putrid," said Hans as he gave us
a tour of the ship. We saw the mess hall, the
Captain's quarters, the poop deck, you name it.

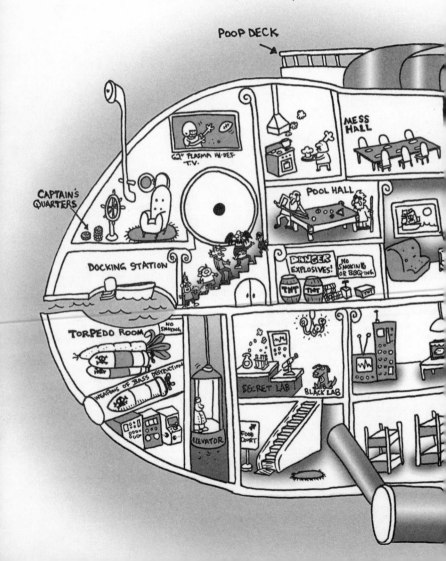

Hans showed us an impressive model of his vessel. "Ve all know zat pollution is ze biggest threat to our beloved lake right now.

"Robo-carp is equipped with a retractable suction device zat vacuums ze pollution and scum from ze bottom of ze lake. I plan to clean up Lake Putrid vithin three months. I call my plan, Operation Scumsucker! I am also currently vorking on a giant scumsucking pig. Look for it in stores next Christmas."

"Jubal," I whispered, "something about this smells funny."

"Are you sure it's not the poop deck?" asked Jubal.

"No," I said. "There's something about Hans I don't trust."

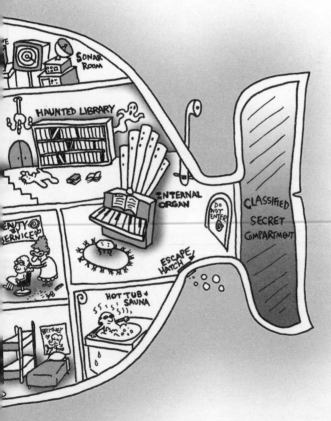

Hans then showed us to our quarters. "In ze morning, ve vill return you to your vorried Gram-mam-ma. For now, rest. I must varn you—stay avay from ze engine room. Robo-carp runs on a top secret and dangerous energy source. In fact, do not leave your rooms. I vouldn't vant any mishaps."

CHAPTER 16

A Pleasant Development

We took Hans's warning very seriously and immediately decided to go exploring. Robo-carp was enormous. There were doors and hallways everywhere.

"Let's try that door right there," said Grampa, "the one that says 'Go Away!' on it."

So we went inside and found...

Hans had the biggest fish tank I've ever seen and in it must have been almost every fish in Lake Putrid!

"Something's not right!" I said.

Then I found Hans's blueprints for a new, swanky development called Lake Pleasant.

"I think I've figured it out!" I said. "Hans is digging his fancy new Lake Pleasant while he scares everyone away from Lake Putrid with this phony monster bass and steals all of the fish with that scumsucking vacuum attachment. Hans is just a lying, greedy, evil fishnapper!"

"Well, nobody's perfect," said Grampa.

"Vell, Vell, vell!" said Hans. "I vas going to invite you to play Parcheezy and instead, I find you've been snooping around! Yes, it's true. Lake Pleasant vill be ze new vacation destination in Gingham County and ze tourists vill spend all zeir money in my hotels, restaurants, and doggy day cares. Lake Putrid vill dry up and die. Vhat good is a fishless, polluted lake haunted by a monster bass?

"Now I have to decide vhat to do vith you. Torture perhaps? Maybe…termination?"

"My vote's for Parcheezy!" said Grampa.

CHAPTER 17

Hanging Around Fish Organs

Before we knew it, we were hanging from the rafters in Hans's music room.

"Vhile my grandson beats you vith a piñata stick, I shall entertain you vith some organ music," said Hans maniacally. "Vhat vould you like to hear? Some disco? How 'bout 'Who Let Ze Dogs Out?'"

MERLE GNAWING ON ROPES

"All this time I thought Hans was just a good foot doctor," said Grampa. "Who knew he was such an accomplished psychopath?"

Suddenly, Hans's organ music was interrupted by a loud alarm. An unidentified object was approaching! Hans whipped out his periscope and scanned the horizon.

Meanwhile, Merle started to gnaw on our ropes.

"Zere is a triangle of large elderly vomen approaching!" said Hans.

"Sounds like your Gramma," said Grampa.

While Hans was distracted, Merle finished gnawing through the ropes and we made our escape.

But first we had to make a stop and release the scaly citizens of Lake Putrid.

We found the escape hatch in the rear of the
Robo-carp and we plopped into the lake.

"This is strangely degrading," said Jubal.

Just as we suspected, Gramma had come to the rescue and she was perched atop the reunited Gingham County female waterskiing team!

And boy, was she was angry! "I'm gonna teach that fish a lesson!" she bellowed as they sped toward the Robo-carp.

The robot fish readied its torpedoes, did a quick
U-turn, and was heading straight for Gramma,
when the unthinkable happened!

Cleta Van Snout's artificial hip suddenly gave
out! The Ladies of the Lake went flying!

Gramma launched into the air like a mighty albatross!

Then she grabbed hold of a latch on the side of the fish.

Gramma accidentally moved the latch, opening up a large compartment. About 2,563 AA batteries spilled out into the lake!

"So that's Robo-carp's secret energy source," Grampa said, disappointed.

CHAPTER 18

Sayonara Robo-carp!

The clunky metal fish was powerless without its batteries, and it quickly capsized.

"You have not seen ze last of me!" shouted Hans as the Robo-carp sank. "I vill be back! And next time I'm bringing a giant metal chicken! Or perhaps a salamander!"

"How did you ever find us?" I asked Gramma.

Gramma held up Paco's fishbowl. "We used Paco to track your trail of Pork Cracklins all the way to that island full of nice hippies. They told us we could find you in the belly of a giant metal fish!"

"Wow!" I said. "A Cracklin-trackin' goldfish!"

"So I guess it was Hans's fish that has been scaring folks these last few years," I continued. "I wonder whatever happened to the real Moby Fizz?"

"I can't help but feel a little silly," said Grampa. "My crazed obsession with finding that fish put everyone in danger. Moby Fizz is just a faded memory, like tiny bubbles in a bottle of flat black-cherry soda."

Once again, the water around Grampa began to churn with bubbles.

"Let me guess," I said. "You had a third can of chili for lunch."

"Nope," said Grampa. "As much as I'd like to take credit for these bubbles, it wasn't me."

CHAPTER 19

Will the Real Moby Fizz Please Stand Up?

Suddenly, the real Moby Fizz surfaced beneath us, and let me tell you, after 60 million years, his breath was kickin'!

Grampa jumped onto the bloated beast and flailed away!

"This is for Captain Froggy!" he yelled as he smacked Moby with his bony arms.

The Ladies of the Lake struck back at Moby in
their famous Swooping Falcon formation.

But the monster put up a fortified force field of fish breath that stopped them in their tracks.

Not even Merle's sofa-ripping cat claws could penetrate Moby's thick hide.

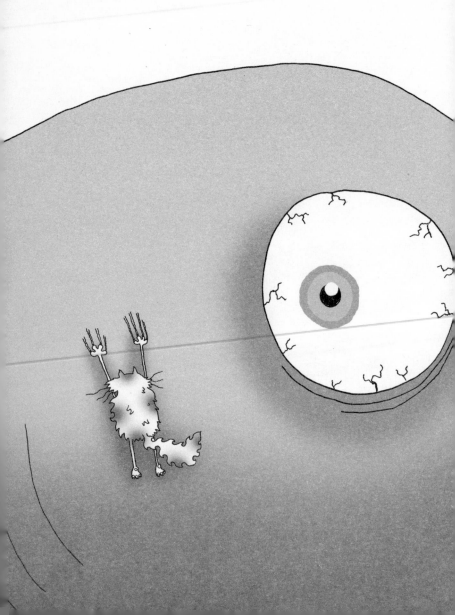

The fishy foe leaped into the air, and his mammoth body was going to crash directly on us!

"Well this it, boys," said Gramma. "I only wish I could've lived to yell at your Grampa for getting us into this mess!"

As a last resort, I held up Paco's fishbowl.

"You wouldn't harm a fellow fish, would you?"
I pleaded.

That's when the strangest thing happened—
Paco jumped up and communicated with Moby.
It kinda sounded like a chipmunk on helium.

Whatever Paco said, it stopped Moby dead in his tracks. He got a sad look on his face, turned around, and swam away.

Moby resurfaced briefly and gently let out a tremendous fish burp. A mysterious object was dislodged by the burp and it flew straight toward us.

The object landed with a splat in Grampa's arms. It was Captain Froggy!

CHAPTER 20

Reunited and It Feels So Slimy

"Froggy!" Grampa shouted with glee. "My brave, little, green, fish mucus-covered friend!"

All was well with the world. Froggy was back in Grampa's arms, the Ladies of the Lake were back together, and the lake was putrid again.

"Let's all go home and put on some dry drawers!" shouted Grampa.

So, Moby Fizz wasn't the monster he was made out to be. Captain Gerald confessed, "So okay, my hand didn't get bitten off. I had a splinter that got infected, but that just doesn't sound as cool."

"What about my Dinky?" asked Marjorie Millner.

"Maybe Moby mistook your poodle for a cream puff or a wad of cotton candy when he ate him," said Grampa. "I know I've done it!"

Captain Froggy was placed on the mantel in the living room. Gramma found this highly disgusting.

And Hans and Jurgen were locked up at the Gingham County Institute for Criminal Masterminds and Their Grandchildren.

As for Paco…

Paco achieved his dream of competing in the finals on *America's Most Talented Animals*.

But, unfortunately, he faced some big competition.

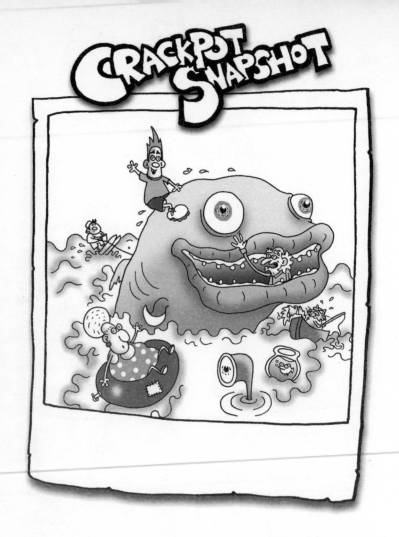

CRACKPOT SNAPSHOT

Something's fishy about this family portrait!
We got double prints at the local photo lab, but
one of the pictures looks wacky. Help us figure
out the differences.

The answers are on the next page. Anyone who cheats will walk the plank, sleep with the fishes, and mow the lawn!